Animals should definitely <u>not</u> act like people.

Written by Judi Barrett and drawn by Ron Barrett

Aladdin Paperbacks

First Aladdin Paperbacks edition 1985
Second Aladdin Paperbacks edition 1989

Story copyright © 1980 by Judith Barrett
Illustrations copyright © 1980 by Ron Barrett

Aladdin Paperbacks
An imprint of Simon & Schuster Children's Publishing Division
1230 Avenue of the Americas
New York, NY 10020

Printed in Hong Kong
10   9   8   7

Library of Congress Cataloging-in-Publication Data

Barrett, Judi.
Animals should definitely not act like people.

Summary: Depicts the inconveniences animals would be burdened with if they behaved like people.
1. Animals—Juvenile humor.   2. Animal behavior—Pictorial works.   3. American wit and humor,
Pictorial. [1. Animals—Wit and humor]   I. Barrett, Ron, ill. II. Title
[PN6231.A5B36   1989]   818'.5402   88-7821
ISBN 0-689-71287-1

Animals should definitely not act like people...

because it would be preposterous for a panda,

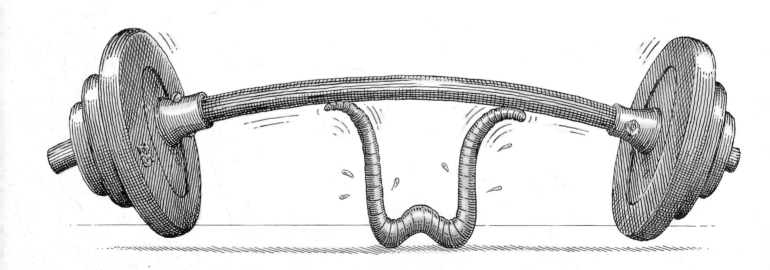

because a
worm would be
worn out,

because it would be outrageous for an octopus to play outfield,

because it
would be
foolish for
a fish,

because a
hippopotamus
would have to
have a heap
of help,

because it
would not pay
for a pigeon,

because a fly
would find
his furniture
falling,

because it
would be
dreadfully dull
for a dog,

because a giraffe would gasp when she glanced to the ground,

because it
would be
troublesome to
a turtle in a
thundershower,

because it
would be so
silly for a
sheep,

because an
ostrich would
look odd,

because a ladybug would have a large load to lift,

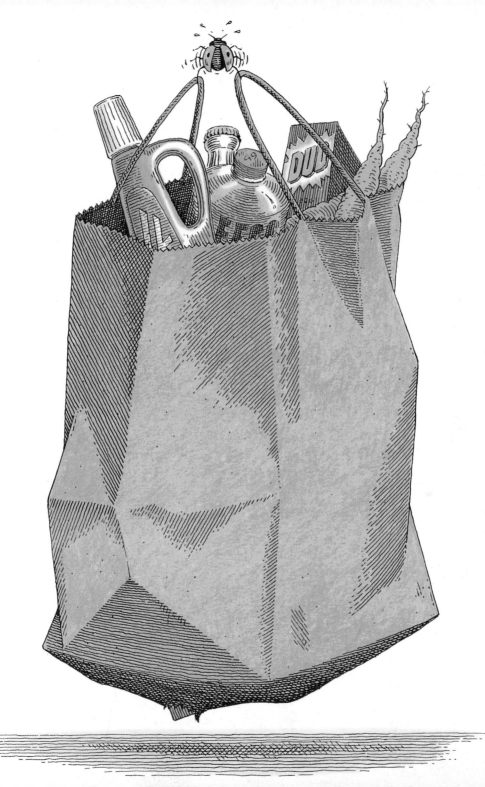

and most of all, because we wouldn't like it!